ANI'S LIGHT

Written by
TANU SHREE SINGH, PhD

Illustrated by
SANDHYA PRABHAT, MA

Magination Press • Washington, DC • American Psychological Association

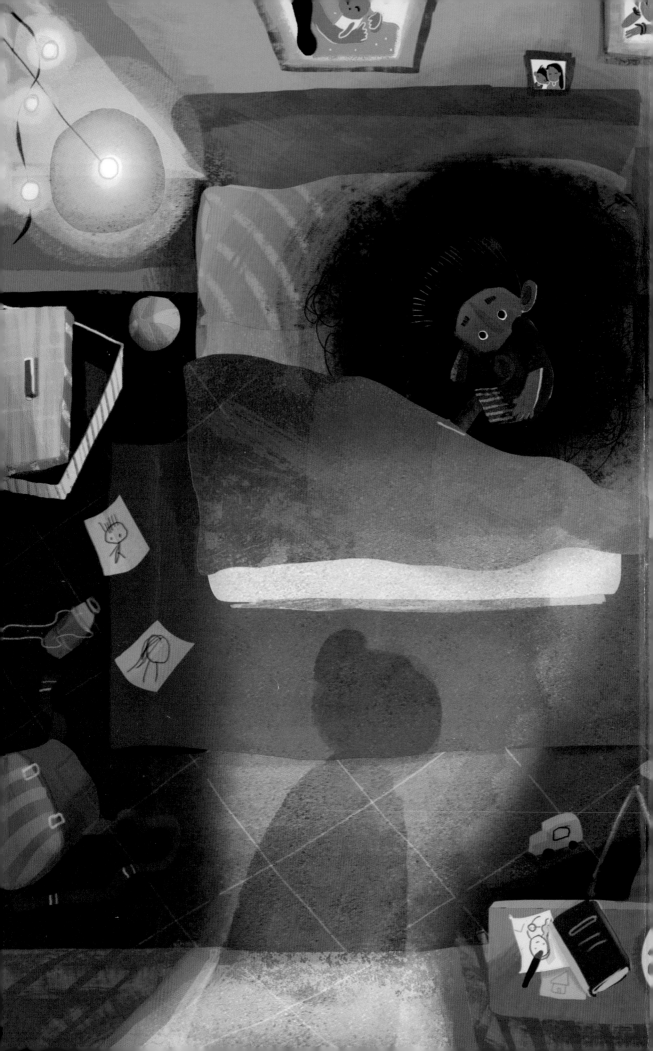

On a night when
the moon shone
and little specks
of light danced
on the ceiling,
Ani lay awake.

"It's dark,"
he said.

When morning came
and the sun peeped in,
he whispered,

"It's dark.
Still dark."

"What a bright, sunny day it is!"
said Nani. "Just right for
some ice cream!"

"Woof!" said Dobby.

Ani said nothing.

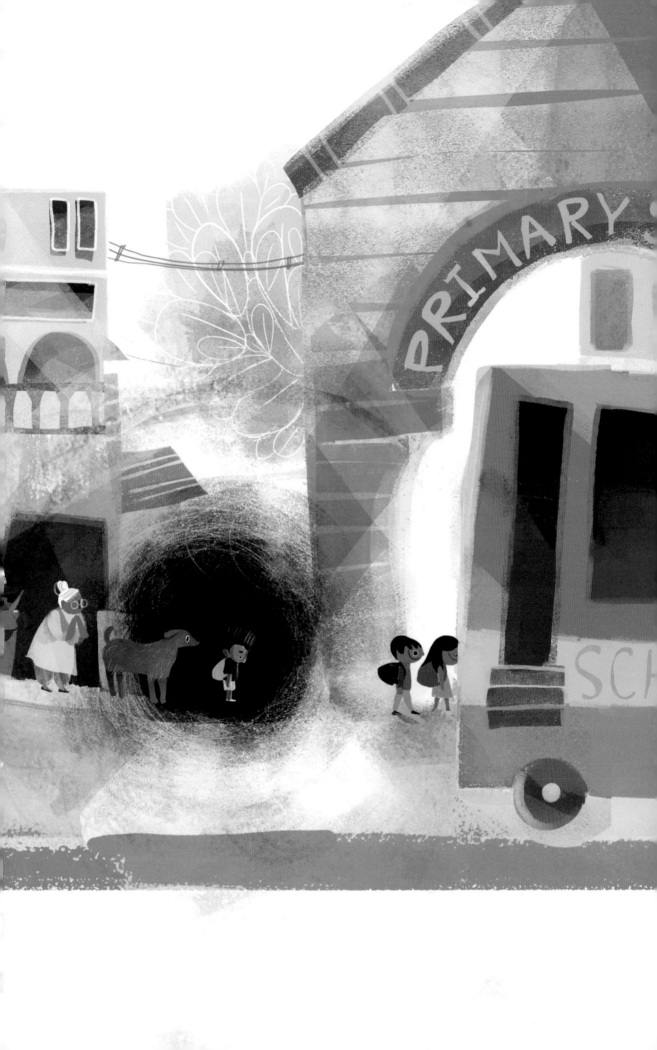

Everything had lost its color.

Even the walk
back home seemed
l-o-n-g-e-r.

Evening came.
Ani still wanted to be left alone.
Why didn't anyone understand?

"Go away!" said Ani.
His friends didn't know
what to do.

Ani didn't either.

"I just want her to come back, Dobby."

Ani was dragging
himself home
when he saw
the light.

He froze.

A car.
Could it be
that car?

It HAD
to be!

Ani ran in.

Without pausing for a breath,
he shot straight into her arms.

Mama's hair was gone.

But she was home, and
nothing was dark anymore!

"I was scared you'd never come back."
"I'm here now." Mama held Ani.
"And so are Dobby, Nani, and
your friends."

"But…" Ani's voice trailed off
as he tried not to cry.

"As long as you let others
love you," Mama said,
"you will be okay."

Ani dug his face into her singing
heartbeat and whispered,
"Even if you aren't there?"

"Yes."

A gentle breeze kissed them both
as he dozed off, mumbling,
"Your hair…can I shave mine, too?"

Mama smiled and held him tighter.

When the morning came
and the sun shone in,
Ani sprang up and said,

"Dust fairies!
Mama,
look!"

Ani and his Mama began this new day
with a kiss and a smile.

For now, Ani had his light.

And all the colors that
the world had for him.

Note to Parents and Caregivers

Fear can be debilitating for children, especially when it arises from a situation like parental illness or another major change that increases their vulnerability. Our first instinct in such a situation is to want to protect the child by keeping the truth from them or creating tall tales. Though we assume they will not understand, hiding the truth rarely helps. Instead, keep the following points in mind to guide a child through difficult situations with empathy, caring, and honesty:

Honesty matters. Children have a built-in lie detector, so it's best not to lie to the child or hide basic information. Whatever the situation, share information in age-appropriate words. There are many books for children that deal with all sorts of difficult topics, including illness, loss, divorce, and more: these can be a great starting point for conversation. For example, if the parent is dealing with cancer, books on that theme would be immensely helpful in explaining the disease and its effects to a child.

It is okay to not know the answers. Some questions have no clear answers, but don't avoid them. It is okay to not know, and even better to address and accept the uncertainty together. As a parent, sometimes we overwhelm ourselves with the need to give factual answers. However, questions around death and uncertainty may have no clear answers. To accept that with the child is to take a step closer to healing.

Help the child deal with their emotions. Acceptance of emotions is an important part of healing and promoting resilience. Let the child know all emotions are acceptable. It is also essential for them to know that bad things can happen in life and it is no one's fault. Learning how to cope and manage their feelings is what will make the difference.

Routines are important. Routines give a sense of security to the child. A consistent schedule and familiar faces create a sense of normalcy. Stick to regular patterns, from bedtimes to school routines, as much as you can.

Plan for fun. The child does need a break. Sometimes we get so caught up in managing problems that we forget that children need doses of fun. Try to schedule some free time together.

Seek help. Life gets overwhelming when illness or huge changes are taking up all our time and energy. In such situations, we need to be vigilant and seek professional help as needed.

Ultimately, the heart and mind have an enormous capacity to heal. All we can do as a parent is to be there and help the child learn to see love, grow resilience, and be reassured that letting the light in can help them through dark times.

To my friend Vaani Arora. Who knew a phone call would become a book!
To the three men in my life. You make everything possible.
To my friend, philosopher, and editor, Richa Jha. You made this shine.
And my parents who believe I am a bestseller.

-TSS

To Richa Jha. For being patient while I painted.
For being kind throughout.
For bringing the best out of the pages.

-SP

Books for Kids From the
American Psychological Association
maginationpress.org

Magination Press is a registered trademark of the American Psychological Association.
Order books at maginationpress.org or call 1-800-374-2721.
Book design by Rachel Ross
Printed by Phoenix Color, Hagerstown, MD

Library of Congress Cataloging-in-Publication Data
Names: Singh, Tanu Shree, author. | Prabhat, Sandhya, illustrator.
Title: Ani's light / by Tanu Shree Singh; illustrated by Sandhya Prabhat.
Other titles: Darkless
Description: Washington, DC : Magination Press, 2020. | "American
Psychological Association." | Summary: Ani's world has gone dark in his
mother's absence, and his family and friends are unable to help, but
when Mama finally returns, with her hair missing, her love chases the
darkness away. Includes a note to parents and caregivers.
Identifiers: LCCN 2019056336 | ISBN 9781433832772 (hardcover)
Subjects: CYAC: Depression, Mental—Fiction. | Mothers and sons—Fiction. |Sick—Fiction.
Classification: LCC PZ7.1.S56813 Ani 2020 | DDC [E]—dc23
LC record available at https://lccn.loc.gov/2019056336

Manufactured in the United States of America
10 9 8 7 6 5 4 3 2 1